BLOB

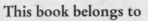

This book belongs to

....

I celebrated *World Book Day 20* with this brilliant
gift from my local bookseller, HarperCollins,
David Walliams and Tony Ross.

Previously written by David Walliams:

THE BOY IN THE DRESS

MR STINK

BILLIONAIRE BOY

GANGSTA GRANNY

RATBURGER

DEMON DENTIST

AWFUL AUNTIE

GRANDPA'S GREAT ESCAPE

THE WORLD'S WORST CHILDREN

THE MIDNIGHT GANG

Also available in picture book:

THE SLIGHTLY ANNOYING ELEPHANT

THE FIRST HIPPO ON THE MOON

THE QUEEN'S ORANG-UTAN

THE BEAR WHO WENT BOO!

THERE'S A SNAKE IN MY SCHOOL!

First published in Great Britain by
HarperCollins *Children's Books* in 2017
HarperCollins *Children's Books* is a division of
HarperCollins*Publishers* Ltd,
HarperCollins Publishers
1 London Bridge Street
London SE1 9GF

The HarperCollins website address is:
www.harpercollins.co.uk
1

ISBN 978–0–00–822153–9

Typeset in Stempel Garamond 11/17pt
Printed and bound in England by Clays Ltd, St Ives plc

David Walliams

BLOB

Illustrated by Tony Ross

HarperCollins *Children's Books*

INTRODUCTION
BY RAJ

Dear Sir/Madam,

I received your letter. The answer is NO. I do NOT want to write an introduction to **Mr Willybum's** new book, *Blob*. How can you even call a book that? **That's not a title!** Even if you sold it for one pound it would be a complete **rip-off.** I do not like **Mr Willybum's** books at all. They are all utter **rubbish!** My pet hamster Shaan could do better. I much prefer Ronald

Dahl. As does Shaan. **Please do NOT EVER EVER EVER** write to me again.

Yours angrily,
Raj

P.S. I HAVE SOME VERY GOOD DEALS ON CHOCOLATE ADVENT CALENDARS. THEY SAY **BEST BEFORE JANUARY 1983** ON THEM, BUT I AM SURE THEY WILL BE FINE. THE CHOCOLATE HAS GONE WHITE BUT YOU COULD ALWAYS SAY IT WAS **WHITE CHOCOLATE** ALL ALONG.

Would you like to meet the characters in the story?

Bob is a ten-year-old boy who lives in a tiny flat with his grandpa. Bob has been told he has a funny face.

This is **Grandpa**. He has been told he has a funny face too. The old man loves his grandson very much, and all he wants is for Bob to be happy. Grandpa is very poor and wishes he had more money to treat his grandson to nice things, like days out together.

Stubbs goes to the same school as Bob. He is a surprisingly short bully.

Stubbs's gang has two other members, **Gaz** and **Baz**. It doesn't matter who is who, as they are so thick even they don't know.

Miss Veer is the harassed headmistress at Grottington School, where Bob is a pupil.

Winston is the kindly old zookeeper at the local zoo. He has worked there all his life and thinks of the animals as his friends. They think of him as their friend too as he feeds them, cleans them, and even clears up their droppings.

Sir Basil Basildon is the incredibly grand owner of the zoo. He always wears a safari suit with a cravat.

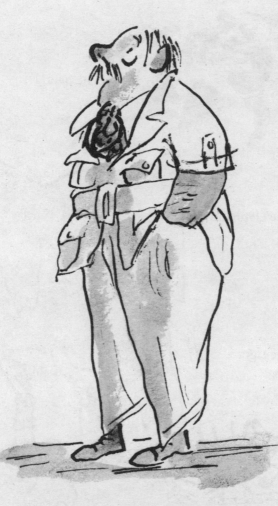

Sir Basil's Zoo is home to animals of all shapes and sizes. There are many you might expect to see. Some of the most popular animals are:

The panda.

The elephant.

The tiger.

The zebra.

And of course, the penguins.

But there are also many animals at Sir Basil's Zoo that you might not expect to see. This story is about one such animal. It's a fish with a funny face, called a blobfish.

This is a map of the zoo, so you can see where all the animals live:

Let's begin the story…

For Stella and Bea
with lots of love
David

CHAPTER ONE

FUNNY FACE

Bob had a funny face. At least, that was what some of the other children at his school told him. Sometimes they used more hurtful words than "funny". Sometimes they called Bob "Blob".

Bob was born with his funny face. He had lived with it for all of his ten years. In fact, he came from a family of funny faces. His grandpa, who he lived with in the old man's tiny flat, had a funny face too. You could trace the funny faces back for generations.

The boy knew his funny face made him stand out at school, and often it made him feel shy.

Grandpa would tell his grandson, "Be proud of your funny face, young Bob. You come from a very long line of funny faces."

But Bob didn't like it one bit. Sometimes he thought having a funny face was the worst thing in the world.

The boy's favourite place was the local zoo. Grandpa would take his beloved grandson there every year as a special treat on Bob's birthday. Together they would marvel at all the animals, and Grandpa would make up funny stories about how they got to look the way they did.

"The elephant has a trunk so she can tap other animals on the shoulder when she's lost and needs to ask for directions."

"The giraffe has a long neck as she's very nosy and likes to look over garden walls."

"The orang-utan grows his hair long because he's a big fan of rock music and likes to headbang."

"The zebra is black and white because he can't make decisions and didn't know what colour he wanted to be."

"Penguins are birds who can't fly themselves as they prefer to travel by aeroplane so they can enjoy the in-flight meal."

The zoo was full of animals with funny faces just like Bob's, so he always felt at home there. His grandpa had long been retired, and barely had enough money to put food on the table, so the pair could only afford to visit the zoo once a year.

This year, however, when Grandpa emptied his piggy bank, it was bad news.

"I'm sorry, Bob," said the old man, as he looked at the three tiny copper coins and one chipped button on the table. "I won't be able to take you to the zoo this year for your birthday."

Bob hid his disappointment. He didn't want to see his grandpa sad. "That's OK. We can always go next year."

"Yes. There's always next year," replied the old man, as he avoided the boy's gaze.

Bob loved his grandpa, but life could be hard because they had no money. All Bob's clothes were a size too small, and his shoes were falling apart.

So on the day of his eleventh birthday, Bob took a detour on his walk home from school, and headed to the zoo. There was a tall tree overlooking the grounds, and Bob climbed it. That way at least he could see his animal friends on his birthday, even from a distance. The boy clung tightly to a branch, and took in the view. He could see all the animals from up there.

Looking down, Bob daydreamed he was piloting a propeller plane flying over the African savanna on a safari. In his dream, he was swooping over herds of magnificent beasts…

"Oi!" came a voice.

It broke the spell cast by the daydream.

"OI!"

Bob looked down. A zookeeper was shouting up at him from the camel's enclosure, bucket and shovel in hand. The old man was standing next to a huge pile of steaming camel dung. The smell snaked up Bob's nostrils, and he steadied himself on the branch of the tree.

"Oi! What are you doing up there, boy?" shouted the zookeeper.

"I fell," lied the boy.

The old man laughed heartily. **"Ha! Ha! Ha!** You can't fall up a tree! Now come on, boy, what are you really doing up there?"

"Nothing," replied Bob. The boy didn't want to get into trouble for stealing a free look at the animals. He wasn't sure if that was a crime or not, but Bob hated getting into trouble.

"You're all the way up a great tall tree, boy!" said the man. "You must be doing something!"

"It's my birthday today. And I always come to the zoo on my birthday."

"Happy birthday!" said the zookeeper.

"Thank you. But this year Grandpa couldn't afford to take me, and I really, really, really wanted to see the animals. I love animals…"

"So do I! Come on down, boy!" said the zookeeper. "I can let you in for free."

"Are you sure?" Bob's eyes widened with excitement.

"Yes! Especially as it's your birthday!"

Bob shimmied down the tree. By the time he'd reached the ground, the keeper had appeared at the back gate of the zoo. He wore dungarees and a friendly smile. There was a whiff of animal dung about him, which was hardly surprising considering his job.

"So, what's your name, young sir?"

"Bob."

"Mr Bob! Welcome back to Sir Basil's Zoo," said the keeper, opening the gate.

The man had a quick look around to make sure nobody had spotted them.

"Thank you so much for this, sir," said the boy.

"Winston! Call me Winston!"

"Thank you, Winston."

"Now come in, Mr Bob! Quick as you like! If the zoo owner spots us, we're both in trouble as big as the biggest hippopotamus dropping. And, trust me, that is big."

"I don't want to get you into any trouble," said Bob, a flash of worry crossing his face.

"You won't if you're quick, Mr Bob. It's a pleasure to meet someone who clearly loves animals as much as I do. Most of our little visitors run straight for the gift shop to buy a dinosaur pencil case. Even though we don't even have any dinosaurs at the zoo! Now, what animals would you like to see today? Let me guess. The tiger?"

"No!"

"The penguins?"

"No!"

"The elephant?"

"No!"

"The zebra?"

"No!"

"The giraffe?"

"No!"

The zookeeper was befuddled. Everyone liked those animals the best, especially the children.

"What then, Mr Bob?"

"I like the animals no one else likes. The ones with the funny faces."

"Good for you, Mr Bob!" exclaimed the

zookeeper. "I bet those would really like a visit. They so often get ignored. Now run along, Mr Bob, before the owner, Sir Basil Basildon, spots you."

"Thank you so much, Winston!"

The boy ran off into the zoo, his heart pounding with excitement.

CHAPTER TWO

LAUGH OR SHRIEK

As usual, Bob's mission was to find those animals in the zoo with the funniest faces. He dashed past the lion, who was standing on a rock so that the wind caught his mane at just the right angle for the visitors' cameras.

"I wonder if he uses shampoo and conditioner or just shampoo?" said a bouffant-haired man.

Bob didn't stop to see the panda either. The black and white bear was sitting chewing on some bamboo and blowing off loudly.

BLURT!

It left a party of old folk from a retirement home befuddled.

"What was that trumpeting sound, dear?" asked an old dear.

"I thought that was you, dear," replied the other old dear.

There was a huge crowd gathered around the elephant. She was spraying water over everyone with her trunk.

"Ooh! This is delightful!" said one posh lady.

"Yes, there's nothing more delightful than showering in freezing-cold water that smells of elephant," said the other.

But Bob just walked on by. He was much more interested in seeing the animals in the zoo who had no visitors crowding around them. These were the ones who many people thought were ugly. They were certainly odd-looking, and Bob found them fascinating. These were the ones he always loved visiting on his birthday trips to the zoo with Grandpa. There was:

Cone-nosed *tapir.*

Aye-aye with her **glowing** *eye-eyes.*

Dugong, or "sea cow".

Elephant seal with his **stumpy** *trunk.*

Hamadryas baboon with *her matching* **red** *face and bottom.*

Hooded seal who could **blow** *his own nose up like a balloon.*

Incredibly slow sloth.

Terrifying *Komodo dragon.*

Marabou stork with his *dingly-dangly neck.*

Pangolin with odd-looking scales all over her back.

Pig-nosed *frog*.

SNAPPING TURTLE.

Proboscis monkey with his **outrageous hooter**.

Spotted handfish.
Was he a hand?
Or was he a fish?

Spiky-backed *echidna*.

Star-nosed mole who looked like he had worms on the end of his face.

Umbrellabird with his long **dangly wattle** that looked like a folded-up umbrella.

Warthog who was half hog, half wart.

When other children passed by these animals, they would either laugh or shriek, neither of which seemed welcome. Looking deep into the eyes of these animals, Bob thought they must be sad. Perhaps it was painful for the "ugly" animals to be ignored while all the "pretty" animals soaked up all the attention?

Bob was particularly intrigued by one creature. Hidden away in a damp, dark corner of the zoo was a little tank.

On the tank was a sign that read:

Blobfish

But inside there was nothing to be seen.

CHAPTER THREE

LURK IN THE MURK

The other visitors to Sir Basil's Zoo ignored the little tank. They were too busy marvelling at the seahorse and the octopus and the clownfish.

"Look! It's the fish from *Finding Nemo*!" said one vicar.

"Is it the actual one from the film?" asked another.

Bob rested his head on the little tank, and peered in. As hard as he looked, he couldn't spot the blobfish anywhere. Perhaps he was hiding behind a rock? Had he buried himself in the sand? Was he lurking in the murky water at the back of the tank? Was he shy? Was he frightened? Did he not like being stared at?

All Bob knew was that the blobfish seemed to be hiding.

Winston the zookeeper passed by the tank on his rounds.

"How are you enjoying yourself, Mr Bob?" he asked.

"I am having the best afternoon, thank you, Winston. I've seen so many interesting animals already."

"Splendid, splendid, splendid."

"But I can't see this one."

Winston put down the bucket of fish he was taking to the penguins. "No. Nobody ever does."

"Is there definitely a fish in there?"

"Definitely, Mr Bob. But I am sorry to say the blobfish hides himself away."

"Why?"

"A couple of years ago, a little girl visited the zoo. When she saw Blob she screamed and projectile-vomited. At the same time."

"Oh no."

"Yes. I had to clean the girl's lunch off the tank. She'd eaten Alphabetti spaghetti. The glass looked like a Scrabble set had exploded all over it."

Indeed, there was a sign now which read:

NO PROJECTILE-VOMITING ON THE GLASS.

"So what happened to the blobfish?"

"The poor little thing was obviously frightened. He hid at the very back of his tank and was never seen again. He won't even eat the food I drop in for him until the dead of night when the zoo is empty."

"That's sad."

"That it is, Mr Bob. I fear you're wasting your time waiting to see that one."

"But I really want to see what a blobfish looks like."

"Good luck, Mr Bob!" said the old man over his shoulder as he left.

Bob wouldn't give up. He waited. And waited. And waited. And then he waited some more.

After an hour, the boy was ready to give up when he noticed another sign at the bottom of the tank. It read:

DO NOT TAP ON THE GLASS!

Like most children (and some grown-ups), when Bob was told NOT to do something, it made him want to do it all the more.*

*Just like seeing these signs often makes you want to do the opposite:

NO RUNNING IN THE CORRIDOR

THIS BED IS NOT A TRAMPOLINE – DO NOT JUMP ON IT

NO BALL GAMES

DO NOT JUGGLE ANTIQUES

WET PAINT. DO NOT SIT HERE

DO NOT PLAY THE CHURCH ORGAN

DO NOT HELP YOURSELF TO CAKES

NO CLIMBING ON THE STATUE

DO NOT FEED THE GORILLAS

OPEN THIS DOOR ONLY IN AN EMERGENCY

In fact, before seeing the "DO NOT TAP ON THE GLASS" sign, Bob had not thought of doing such a thing. It hadn't even crossed his mind. Now he had an overwhelming desire to do it. Bob was curious. What would happen if he tapped on the glass? Would it shatter? Would the zoo self-destruct? Would the world end? There was only one way to find out.

Bob glanced left and right to check no one was looking. Then slowly the boy lifted his knuckles to the tank.

TAP!

Nothing stirred.

TAP!

Again nothing.

TAP! TAP! TAP!

Bob put his face right up against the tank and peered into the murky water. From the other side of the thick glass he must have looked quite a sight, his funny face flattened against it.

At the very back of the tank, Bob could just make out something stirring. It was faint at first – a swirl of water and sand – and then out of the shadows a face appeared.

It was the ugliest face Bob had ever seen. And he had seen some ugly faces – his family photograph album was full of them.

"Arrrrgg

gggh!" screamed the boy.

The blobfish must have been scared too, at the sight of this squashed nose and mouth, and the big bulging eyes staring back at him. The fish's mouth opened and a giant bubble of air burst out. His eyes widened in terror before he retreated to the far side of the tank.

The pair had frightened the life out of each other.

CHAPTER FOUR

A BRUSSELS SPROUT UP EACH NOSTRIL

The next morning at break, Bob stole off to the library. It was his favourite place in the whole of Grottington School. The library offered peace and quiet from the bullies who teased him for his funny face.

Bullies are never into books. Reading makes their brains hurt.

In the corner of the library reserved for books about animals, Bob found what he was looking for:

THE WHOPPING BOOK OF FISH.

It was sandwiched between **THE GINORMOUS GORILLA BOOK** and *THE REALLY TOO BIG BOOK OF ANTS.*

Bob sat cross-legged on the library floor. Skimming past the well-thumbed pages on the deadly fish that children are always drawn to – the sharks, piranhas and stingrays – the boy finally found an entry for the blobfish. In such an enormous book, it seemed unfair that this particular fish was given so little space. It had barely more than a postage-stamp-sized entry. Bob had to squint to read it. In the very few lines of description, Bob learned that the blobfish was a deep-sea fish, with a body made up of jelly. The final sentence in the entry read: "The blobfish is considered to be the ugliest animal in the world."

Bob felt sad for a moment. What an awful thing to be best at – ugliness. It wasn't the fastest, the cleverest, the biggest, the smallest, or the deadliest. It was the ugliest. No wonder nobody who visited Sir Basil's Zoo stopped to look at the thing. Except of course that one little girl who vomited her Alphabetti spaghetti over the tank.

Just as Bob was about to put the book back on the shelf, he felt a long shadow cross his face. Looking up, he realised that looming over him was Stubbs, with his gang behind him.

I say "looming". Stubbs was only slightly taller than Bob when Bob was sitting down. Stubbs was the shortest boy in the whole school. Maybe that's why he turned into a bully, to show everyone how powerful he was, even though he only came up to the teachers' knees. It was as if a ten-tonne truck had been dropped on his head, squashing him. But he was the hardest child in Grottington School, which was full of hard children.

Stubby Stubbs was even harder than:

BRUTAL BRIAN

FIERCE FENELLA

TERRIBLE TAMIKA

NASTY NATALIE

CRUEL COLIN

VICIOUS VICTORIA

ROUGH ROMESH

WICKED WILL

HEARTLESS HELEN

RUTHLESS RUTH

Bob stood up and realised he was now a fair bit taller than Stubbs. Still, Stubbs scared him.

"'Ello, Blob," said the bully.

"HA! HA!" Stubbs's two henchmen Gaz and Baz laughed, even though Stubbs had called Bob "Blob" a thousand times before. It hadn't been funny the first time, let alone now.

"We looked all over school for you," said Stubbs. "What is this strange place? I've never seen it before."

"It's the library," replied Bob.

"What's that all about then?"

"It's a home for books."

"What are they all about then?"

Bob looked around the shelves and shelves of books. "I'm not sure I've got time to go into all that, but it's been smashing to see you three."

The boy tried to pass, but the bullies blocked his path.

"Wot you readin'?" demanded Stubbs, snatching the book off him.

Stubbs's stubby fingers tore at a page – and in his hands was the picture of the blobfish.

"Ha! Ha! Look, boys," began the bully,

"Blob's reading about himself!"

Stubbs's gang of two looked over their leader's shoulder.

"I don't get it," said Baz.

Stubbs looked embarrassed by his gang's thickery, but pressed on.

"Well, we call Bob 'Blob', and this 'ere is a 'blobfish'," he explained.

"Oh yes," said Gaz.

"I still don't get it," said Baz.

Stubbs shook his head wearily, but pressed on with the bullying. He held up the ripped-out page next to Bob's head.

"Spot the difference! Ha! Ha! I can't!" exclaimed Stubbs.

The henchmen looked confused.

"One is a boy..." began Gaz.

"...and that other is a piece of paper with a picture of a fish on it," continued Baz.

Bob sighed. This was just the latest in a long list of horrible things the Stubbs gang had done to him.

There was the time when they put a large spider in between two slices of bread in Bob's lunch box.

Bob would never forget when the gang made him drink tea from his own sock.

Or the time when they buried his homework in the football field.

There was also the time when the gang forced him to eat a cracker smothered in their own foot-cheese.

And who could forget the day when the Stubbs gang made Bob walk around school with a Brussels sprout in each nostril? Poor Bob looked like he had two giant bogies hanging from his hooter.

There was the time when they tricked Bob into thinking it was dress-up day at Grottington School. The boy came dressed as a robot, wrapped in tin foil while everybody else was in school uniform.

And the day when the gang thought it was hilarious to fill his school bag with custard.

One time they put a loo seat over Bob's head and made him pretend to all the other children it was a trendy new scarf.

Bob had got into trouble when they scratched *"BOB WOZ 'ERE"* on the headmistress Miss Veer's office door.

And of course there was the day they made Bob put two footballs down the back of his trousers so it looked like he had a massive inflatable bottom.

"Ha! Ha!" Stubbs pressed on with his joke. "Spot the difference! I can't!"

Bob knew that Stubbs wanted to upset him. Like all bullies, what Stubbs loved was to make his victim cry.

But the boy had an idea. He wouldn't cry. He would laugh!

"HA! HA! HA! HA! HA! HA! HA! HA! HA! HA! HA! HA! HA! HA! HA! HA! HA!"

CHAPTER FIVE

Bob glanced at the picture of his supposed lookalike, the blobfish. Then he screwed up his face to look as much like the world's ugliest animal as possible. He even pretended to blow a bubble of air from his mouth, like the real one had the day before in the zoo.

The two henchmen laughed.

"HA! HA! HA! HA! HA! HA! HA! HA!"

"Now *that* is funny!" said Gaz.

"Can he be in our gang, Boss?" asked Baz.

Stubbs was not amused. He hated that Bob was making his henchmen laugh. It took away his power. And bullies love power.

"Blob! Stop being funny!" ordered Stubbs.

This made Bob want to be funnier and funnier

and funnier. The boy opened his eyes as wide as they would go, picked up the book and put it on his back as if it was a fin.

"STOP IT!"

thundered Stubbs.

But there was no stopping Bob. He brushed past the bullies and pretended to swim around the room, weaving in and out of the bookcases. Soon the other children in the library were laughing too.

"HA! HA! HA!"

Even the rather proper librarian Miss Browse couldn't help but snort. Stubbs looked on with fury as Bob "swam" out of the library, and out of the clutches of the bullies.

As he turned a corner and got his breath back, Bob realised something.

Something important.

He had made something bad into something good.

Stubbs had said he looked like this fish. And maybe he did a little. But by playing up to it, he'd beaten the bullies at their own game.

BRRRING!

As the school bell rang at the end of the day, Bob made his way to Sir Basil's Zoo. Today he skipped all the way there. A brilliant thought had crossed his mind.

PING!

He could try to teach the blobfish the same trick.

CHAPTER SIX

WIGGLE YOUR BOTTOM

Winston the kindly zookeeper sneaked the boy in through the back gate of Sir Basil's Zoo again.

"Welcome, welcome, welcome back, Mr Bob!"

"Thank you so much, Winston. This is so kind of you. Sorry I don't have the money to buy a ticket."

"That's all right. We got away with it once, but we have to be careful. If Sir Basil Basildon sees you coming in this way, we'll both be in deep doo-doo."

"I understand," replied Bob, nodding seriously but trying not to smile at the word "doo-doo".

"So, what animal have you come to see at our little zoo today, Mr Bob?"

"The blobfish!"

"Again?!"

"Yes! I've been reading up all about it in the school library."

"Best of luck spotting our little friend."

"I have an idea to try and get him out of his shell."

Winston looked mightily confused. "But, Mr Bob, the blobfish doesn't have a shell."

"I mean, get him to not be so shy."

"Oh, that would be wonderful! As soon as I've mucked out the hippopotamus, I'll head over."

The boy rushed to the aquarium, past the octopus and the stingray, both of which had crowds of children gathered around them.

As usual, no one was looking at the tank that housed the blobfish. And once again the blobfish was nowhere to be seen.

Bob peered deep into the murky water. Once again he tapped on the glass.

TAP! TAP! TAP!

Nothing.

He tapped harder this time.

TAP! TAP! TAP!

Still nothing.

Bob tapped as hard as could.

TAP! TAP! TAP!

After a few moments, he saw a swirl of sand and slowly the blobfish came into view.

The fish looked timid at first. He hovered at the back of his tank, stealing glances at the boy on the other side of the glass.

Why is this annoying child here again? the fish wondered, and hoped he hadn't been eating Alphabetti spaghetti.

Bob set his plan into action. The boy started to do his best impression of the fish. He widened his eyes and mouth, and pretended to blow bubbles of air.

The fish stared at the boy. What was this strange visitor doing now?

Bob tried again. He widened his eyes and mouth as far as they would go, and blew the biggest bubble he could.

The fish swam right up to the glass.

Then the most incredible thing happened.

The blobfish began copying the boy.

Bob blinked.

Blob blinked.

Bob blew a bubble.

Blob blew a bubble.

Bob twisted and turned.

Blob twisted and turned.

Soon a crowd of children had gathered around the blobfish tank. This was turning into quite a show.

Bob pushed his face right up against the glass.

Blob did the same.

Bob squashed his nose. Blob squashed his nose.

"HA! HA! HA!" The other children were in hysterics.

Winston was busy feeding the piranhas, but hearing all the commotion, the zookeeper huffed and puffed his way over to see what was going on.

A huge smile spread across the old man's face.

"Mr Bob and Mr Blob! The best double act in town!" Winston laughed heartily. "HA! HA! HA! HA! HA!"

The laughter made Bob feel funnier. The boy was on a roll now. He flapped his arms. Blob flapped his fins. Bob floated up. The fish floated up. Bob floated down. Blob floated down.

The children all applauded.

Finally, as an encore, Bob wiggled his bottom. Then Blob wiggled his bottom.

A huge cheer broke out.

"**HOORAY!**" shouted Winston and all the visitors. Bob smiled and took a bow. Then Blob did too.

The boy put his hand up to the thick glass. The fish put his fin up. It was as if they were touching.

Winston put his hand on the boy's shoulder. "In all my years working at the zoo, I have never seen anything so joyous. Well done, boy!"

"Thank you, Winston. But I'm just getting started."

"What do you mean, Mr Bob?" asked the zookeeper.

But before he could answer, the boy was gone...

CHAPTER SEVEN

HONKING HOOTER

Bob's first stop was the proboscis monkey.

He was sitting alone on a branch at the back of his cage, ignoring the world.

"Hello!" called Bob.

The monkey didn't turn round.

"HELLO!" Bob called, louder this time.

The animal hunched his back.

"HELLO!!!"

Bob sighed. Then he had an idea. The boy had a big nose. Not as big as the proboscis monkey's – no one's nose was as big as that – but Bob's nose was still big.

So Bob started honking his hooter. He pressed his nose with his finger and made a loud hooting noise.

"HONK!"

The boy could see the monkey beginning to stir.

"HONK!!!" Bob did it again.

The monkey looked quickly up over his shoulder.

"HONK!!!!!!"

The animal's eyes shone. Slowly he lifted his head. The monkey's outrageous nose dangled free for all to see.

The monkey pressed his own hooter.

"H O N K !"

went Bob.

The animal looked confused for a moment. Then he pressed his nose again.

"HONK!" The boy provided the sound effect again.

The third time the proboscis monkey pushed down on his hooter, he made the honking noise himself.

HONK!

Then the most magical thing happened. The monkey actually laughed to himself.

HA! HA!

He pressed his nose again. **HONK!** And again. **HONK!**

Now the monkey didn't seem shy about having a big nose. He was delighting in it. Instead of hiding it away, he was showing it off for the world to see. Finally the proboscis monkey looked proud to have the dangliest, dongliest nose in the whole of the zoo.

Though there was quite some competition from...

the aardvark...

the toucan...

and the anteater.

A crowd of visitors had previously been gathered around the cute chimpanzees, but now everyone was far more excited to see this funny little monkey with his honking hooter.

As the people were being wowed by this unexpected show, Winston huffed and puffed his way over. But before he had even arrived at the monkey's cage, Bob had run off to find the next animal.

"Wait for me!" called the old zookeeper, hurrying after the boy.

The dugong was floating in her tank, grazing on some seagrass. On the other side of the glass was a group of schoolgirls laughing at the poor creature.

"She looks like a cow!" said one.

"A fat cow!" said another.

"An enormously fat cow!" added a third.

"Ha! Ha! Ha!" the girls all laughed. Oh, how hilarious they thought they were.

The dugong dived down under the water to blot out the sound of the girls' mean mockery.

Bob had an idea: why not beat the girls at their own game? If they thought this animal looked like a cow, then why shouldn't she act like a cow?

He pushed past the girls.

"Do you mind, you little squirt?" shouted one.

The boy ignored her and tapped on the glass to get the dugong's attention. The animal looked the funny-faced boy straight in the eye. But when Bob pointed upwards, gesturing for the dugong to surface, she shook her head. Bob wouldn't give up. He smiled at her, and put his hands together to plead. Finally, the dugong breathed out through her snout as if she was sighing, and came to the surface.

Bob climbed up on to a bench so he could look over the tank. The schoolgirls stared at this funny-faced little boy.

"What on earth is that revolting child doing now?" asked one.

"Moo!" mooed the boy.

The animal regarded the boy with a look of puzzlement on her blubbery face.

"Moo!" mooed Bob again.

The boy then nodded to the dugong that it was her turn. But she remained silent.

"Moo!" mooed the boy, louder this time.

Eventually the dugong mooed back.

Moo!

It was a muffled, watery moo, but a moo nonetheless.

"Moo!" mooed the boy back, as loud as he could.

M*OO!* mooed the dugong. Now she was playing up to her "sea cow" nickname. The schoolgirls who had been cruelly laughing before were now cheering with delight.

"This is so jokes!" remarked one.

Amazingly the animal seemed to smile, and mooed again.

M*OOOOOOO!*

The sound was so loud it echoed all over the zoo. The penguins next door covered their ears with their little wings.

M*OOOOOOOOOOOOO!*

Now the schoolgirls were applauding.

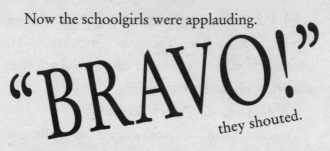

"BRAVO!" they shouted.

Just then, Winston caught up at last, chuckling with delight at the mooing sea cow. "Well done, boy!" he said, looking around for Bob. But Bob had already dashed off...

"WAIT FOR ME!" called out the zookeeper.

CHAPTER EIGHT

SLAP-BANG

In no time, Bob had all the funniest-looking animals in the zoo putting on shows for the crowds.

The boy grabbed an umbrella from a grown-up. He twirled it around, teaching the umbrellabird an old-fashioned dance routine.

Next, the boy pushed his chin down to his chest so his neck bulged out. The marabou stork copied and began proudly showing off his dingly-dangly neck.

Then he had the elephant seal make a trumpeting sound from his stumpy trunk. *PA-PAA!*

The real elephant next door looked most displeased to be beaten at her own game, and went into a giant sulk.

Then Bob put his face up to the aye-aye's cage and made his eyes go as wide as he could. The little lemur copied him, and in no time at all had the zoo visitors jostling for a look.

Following that, Bob pinched his nose and blew into it, making it as big as he could. After a few tries, the hooded seal did the same, to the delight of the crowd.

The sloth was famous for being the slowest animal on earth. The boy taught her to move even slower. The children began playing a game of Grandma's Footsteps with the sloth, turning around to see if she had moved. She hadn't.

Then Bob lifted his nose and marched up and

down outside the tapir's enclosure. The animal followed the boy, pushing her huge cone-shaped nose proudly into the air for all to see.

Next, the boy showed the warthog how to preen herself as if she was the most beautiful creature on earth. Soon she was posing for the cameras like a supermodel.

He taught the snapping turtle to open her mouth wide and then snap it shut as fast as she could.

SNAP!
SNAP!

The zoo visitors were mightily impressed by this strange-looking creature's skill.

After that, Bob grabbed a handful of straws from the zoo café and stuck them to the back of his school blazer with chewy sweets. The boy raced over to the echidna's enclosure, and jumped down on to all fours. The animal looked on curiously, and Bob began arching his back. The echidna did the same, proudly showing off his marvellous long white spikes.

Racing off to the next cage, Bob put his hand over his nose and flicked his fingers in and out. This encouraged the star-nosed mole to show off his most unusual hooter.

Next, Bob coaxed the spotted handfish out from behind a rock, by gliding his hand across the glass. In no time it was as if the boy's hand and the fish were swimming together, and the crowd was marvelling at this marvellous creature.

Soon after, the boy found the pangolin. Bob rolled himself up into a ball and the animal copied him, creating the biggest pine cone the world had ever seen.

A bottom as bright red as a tomato is nothing to be ashamed of. In fact, it should be celebrated. Bob wiggled his bottom in front of the hamadryas baboon's cage. The monkey needed little encouragement, and soon was putting on the best bottom-wiggling show ever seen.

The Komodo dragon looked like a dinosaur. *Children love dinosaurs*, thought Bob. All he had to do was make the lizard act like a dinosaur. So he taught her to roar like one.

Soon the dragon's roar was so loud it could be heard all over the zoo. This was much to the annoyance of the tiger, who had always thought of herself as the best at roaring.

There was just one more animal, thought Bob. Flushed with the thrill of it all, Bob raced off to find him. But not looking where he was going – the boy ran slap-bang into a grown-up.

"OOF!"

His funny face bounced off the man's fat tummy.

"What do you think you're doing, boy?" came an angry voice.

The boy looked up. It was the zoo owner, Sir Basil Basildon.

CHAPTER NINE

AN ELEPHANT ATE IT

"I was j-j-just…" spluttered Bob.

"Spit it out, boy!" boomed Sir Basil. The man's voice echoed around his zoo.

"I was just trying to help the animals, sir."

"Well, you are NOT helping!" The zoo owner's face was red with rage. "Making my fish pull funny faces. Encouraging a monkey to squeeze his own nose as if it was a hooter. Now you're teaching an animal who isn't supposed to moo to MOO! Whatever next? Are you going to teach a frog to oink?"

"Yes, sir. That's exactly what I was going to do. The pig-nosed frog."

This only enraged Sir Basil further. "I don't want you in my zoo ever again!"

"B-b-but, sir…"

"Let me see your ticket, boy."

Bob panicked. "An elephant ate it!"

Sir Basil's already narrow eyes narrowed.

"A likely story! So you didn't even pay to get into my zoo? Right. I'm calling the police!"

"**DON'T!**" someone shouted.

Bob and Sir Basil turned round. Winston the zookeeper was standing just a few paces away, a bucket of fish in his hand.

"How dare you shout at me?" bellowed the owner.

"I'm sorry, sir," spluttered Winston. He was nervous of Sir Basil, as was everyone who worked at the zoo. "But I had to explain. There's no need to call the police."

"Why not? This nasty little runt has sneaked into MY zoo without paying."

The boy looked up at the zookeeper. He didn't know what to say or do.

"Mr Bob didn't sneak in," replied Winston.

"Then would you care to explain how he got in here without a ticket?"

There was silence for a moment before the zookeeper mumbled, "I let the boy in for free."

"YOU ARE FIRED!" bellowed Sir Basil. "I want you both out of my zoo this instant!"

"Please, please, please don't sack him, sir!" pleaded the boy. "Winston loves these animals."

"I don't care.

OUT!"

The friends shared a despairing look. Then Winston and Bob made their way towards the front gate as the crowds of visitors looked sadly on.

"I am so sorry," said the boy.

"It wasn't your fault, Mr Bob," replied the ex-zookeeper.

Bob bowed his head, as he held on to the old man's hand.

All around the zoo, the animals stopped and watched.

HONK! came a sound.

The boy looked up. It was the proboscis monkey honking his hooter.

HONK! He did it again.

The dugong let out a ginormous *MOOOO.*

The echidna put up his spikes. *PRING!*

The elephant seal trumpeted through his trunk.

PA-PAA!

The snapping turtle snapped again and again and again.

The Komodo dragon roared the biggest dinosaur roar she could. It would have frightened a *Tyrannosaurus rex.*

CLUNK! CLUNK! CLUNK! CLUNK!

The pangolin rolled up into a pine cone and bowled herself around her enclosure, knocking down everything in sight.

The hooded seal blew up his nose. **TOOT! TOOOOOT!**

The marabou stork dingle-dangled his dingly-dangly neck.

DINGLE DANGLE

The warthog snorted. **HHMPH!**

The cone-nosed tapir put her cone-nose as high as she could in the air.

TWANG!

The aye-aye made her eyes **glow** as bright as she could. DING! DING!

The umbrellabird trilled and twirled. TWOO! TWOO!

The spotted handfish started clicking his fins together as if they were fingers. CLICK! CLICK!

The hamadryas baboon wiggled her bright red bottom. WIGGLE! WAGGLE!

HONK! TWANG! CLICK!

The sloth, however, remained perfectly still.

As for the blobfish, he swam up out of the water with all his might and performed the most incredible jump. At the highest point, he stopped still in the air for a moment and let out a ginormous...

BBB

BUUUURRRPPP!

...before splashing back down into his tank with a massive SPLOSH!

The sound of all the animals protesting was deafening.

"WHAT ON EARTH IS HAPPENING?"

boomed Sir Basil.

"It's the animals, sir. They're revolting!" replied Winston.

CHAPTER TEN

PIGTASTIC

"I know they're revolting!" bellowed Sir Basil. "Just look at how revoltingly ugly they are."

"They're rebelling, I mean. And they're not ugly, sir," spoke up Bob. "They're beautiful! Look!"

The boy's words stopped the zoo owner in his tracks. Sir Basil was amazed. All the animals who were normally ignored had crowds gathered around them.

"How did this happen?" asked Sir Basil, looking mightily confused.

The boy smiled, but was too shy to speak up for himself. His friend Winston took over.

"It was all thanks to this young boy here. Mr Bob loves this zoo, but his grandpa can only afford to take him once a year. It's his absolute favourite place to go. So I let him in without a ticket."

"Mmm…" Sir Basil sounded unconvinced that allowing someone into his zoo for free could ever be a good idea.

"He loves the animals who most of the other visitors to the zoo completely ignore."

"The blobfish especially," piped up Bob, adding sadly. "The bullies at my school said I looked like it."

The zoo owner studied the boy for a moment. "Hmm. Yes. I can see the resemblance."

"They call me 'Blob'," added Bob. "I've always had a funny face. I come from a family of funny faces. My grandpa has a funny face, as did all his relatives. I suppose that's why I feel so at home in the zoo around the animals. It's full of funny faces."

"Who are these bullies?" asked Winston kindly.

"Oh, just some boys at my school." The boy looked down at his feet.

"I'd like to meet them!" replied the zookeeper, a look of anger flashing across his face.

"Me too!" said Sir Basil. His eyes were wet with tears at the boy's sad story. "I'd like to give them a piece of my mind. Now, Blob... I am terribly sorry, I mean Bob. Bob. Not Blob. Bob. Now, Blob, I don't think you need to leave my zoo after all."

"No?" asked the boy.

"No. In fact, I would like to offer you and your grandfather lifetime passes to my zoo."

"**WOW! THANK YOU, SIR!**" said Bob. He felt so happy he wanted to sing or dance.

"Half-price entry. Except weekends."

Bob looked glum. His grandpa lived on a measly pension, so they still wouldn't be able to afford tickets.

Sir Basil looked at the boy, and sighed. "All right then. FREE!"

"YES!" exclaimed Bob, jumping up and down with excitement.

There were murmurs of interest from the crowd of visitors who had gathered around the three.

"But just so you know, everyone," said Sir Basil, addressing the crowd, "this is very much a one-off!"

People murmured and tutted before moving on to catch a glimpse of all these beautiful animals the boy had befriended.

"And, Winston, you can keep your job."

"THANK YOU, SIR!" exclaimed the zookeeper.

"But you are not to let anyone else in for free. Ever, ever, ever. Do you understand me?"

"Yes, sir."

"Good. Now back to work!"

"Yes, sir!"

Bob put his hand up. "What about the pig-nosed frog, sir?"

"What about it, boy?"

"Well, I never had the chance to see it. It's the frog none of the visitors come to see as it has a rather unusual nose."

"Yes. It's more of a snout, hence the name, 'pig-nosed frog'."

"Well, I think it's time we taught it to **oink**."

"We?" asked Sir Basil, arching an eyebrow.

"Yes. We."

It was quite something, seeing Sir Basil Basildon down on his hands and knees in the mud. He had joined Winston and Bob beside the tank of the rarely seen pig-nosed frog. As if having a pig nose wasn't enough, this frog was also purple and rather chubby. She looked like she'd been inflated. Indeed, the frog might be mistaken for a balloon.

The poor animal had been laughed at or screamed at so many times, she now spent most of her time hiding behind a rock at the back of her tank.

However, the rock she hid behind wasn't quite big enough. The trio could clearly make out a big purple bottom sticking out at one end.

Bob pushed his face up against the glass. **"Oink!"** went the boy. **"Oink! Oink!"** The purple pig-nosed frog didn't move.

Winston joined in. **"Oink! Oink!"**

The creature stayed still.

The pair looked at Sir Basil for help.

"I'm not sure this is such a good idea," he pleaded.

"The frog needs all our encouragement, sir," replied Bob. "Please!"

Reluctantly, the man began to **oink** like a pig. He wasn't very good at it. In fact, his **oink**s sounded posh. *"Oinking. Oinking."*

However, the purple pig-nosed frog must have been intrigued at this strange sound, as her head popped up from behind the rock at the back of her tank. At first only her eyes were visible.

Sir Basil looked at the boy. "What now?"

"Again! Again!" said Bob.

The zoo owner took a deep breath, before beginning again. *"Oinking. Oinking."*

"Louder!" whispered Winston.

"OINKING! OINKING!" carried on Sir Basil, rather getting the hang of it now. *"OINKING! OINKING!"*

Now the whole head of the frog popped up from behind the rock, revealing her pigtastic nose.

Oinking! she oinked.

It was faint at first. Then she oinked again.

Oinking! A little louder this time.

Bob looked behind him. A crowd of Cub Scouts had gathered around the tank, all no doubt wondering what on earth was going on.

OINKING!

Sir Basil looked startled as the frog leaped out from behind her rock and landed right in front of the man's face.

OINKING! oinked the frog.

"OINKING!" oinked Sir Basil back.

Soon the crowd were oinking too, which delighted the frog no end. The more they oinked, the more the frog oinked. As more and more people gathered to join in the fun, it was clear that the purple pig-nosed frog was going to be another star attraction.

Sir Basil stumbled to his feet. Winston steadied him with his arm.

"Thank you," said Sir Basil. "And thank YOU, young Bob, for all you've done for my zoo. So when will we see you again?"

Bob thought for a moment. "On Friday the school is coming here on a trip. I was going to be the only one not going because my grandpa couldn't afford it. But now I have my free pass I can come too!"

"Wonderful! Hang on a moment." A thought seemed to occur to Sir Basil. "Are these bullies you spoke of coming too?"

Bob looked sorrowful. Stubbs and his henchmen could be relied upon to ruin every school trip for him.

There were the occasions when:

They fed Bob's clothes to a goat at a farm, so he had to spend the whole trip in his undercrackers.

They hooked the boy's trousers on to the end of a stalactite in a cave and left him there.

They dismantled LEGOLAND so they could bury Bob in a mountain of plastic bricks.

The bullies made Bob climb to the very top of a *Tyrannosaurus rex* skeleton.

They tied him to the tracks at a miniature railway.

"HELP!"

They stuffed him into a cannon at a fort and fired it.

KABOOM!

They made Bob go down an indoor ski slope on his bottom, and the seat of his trousers caught fire.

"ARGH!"

They stole the costume off a dummy at Hampton Court Palace, and then dressed Bob up as Queen Elizabeth I.

The bullies wrapped the boy in brown paper and put a stamp on him and posted him to Siberia.

They pushed him into a vat of rhubarb yoghurt at a factory.

They locked him in a glass case at the Natural History Museum with some waxworks of cavemen. Poor Bob was trapped in there for a week.

"Yes, sir, the bullies will be coming," replied Bob with a heavy heart. "The entire school is coming."

"Splendid!" exclaimed Sir Basil. "Then we must lay on something special for them."

"Oh yes, sir!" said the zookeeper, smiling.

Bob knew the grown-ups were up to something. He just didn't know what. Yet.

Needless to say, Bob couldn't wait for Friday to come. Not only was the zoo his favourite place to visit, but he also knew there was a surprise in store for the bullies who had made his life such a misery for so long.

As the headmistress Miss Veer led the schoolchildren into the zoo, Stubbs made sure he was right behind Bob.

"Blob! Ha! Ha! That's your name! Blob!"

Bob said nothing, and smiled to himself. Stubbs and his two henchmen, Baz and Gaz, were baffled.

The schoolchildren were fascinated with all the unusual-looking animals who Bob had worked his magic on. These were the ones who were entertaining the crowds now, while the lion, the gorilla and the giraffe all looked on, sulking.

The children from Bob's school gathered excitedly around the pangolin, who was showing off her scales.

"Come along now, children!" announced Miss Veer. "Don't you want to see the tiger?"

"No, miss!" piped up one little girl. "The tiger is boring. She just lies there sunning herself. Look at this funny little chap!"

As the bullies flicked Bob's ears with their fingers and sniggered, out of the corner of his eye the boy spotted a figure standing high up on top of the aviary, where the zoo's birds were kept. At first Bob thought that the bullies might have put someone up there. It was the kind of thing they did. But then the boy realised it was Sir Basil Basildon. What was the zoo owner doing?

There he was standing with his legs akimbo, his suit trousers flapping in the wind. The man was looking through a pair of binoculars. After a moment, he made a signal with his arm to Winston, who had appeared right by the pangolin's enclosure.

Winston winked at Bob.

Bob smiled at Winston.

The boy was bursting with excitement. He knew something big was coming, but what?

Then, to the schoolchildren's horror, the zookeeper did something unexpected – he opened the enclosure gate. They all hurried back and huddled together. The headmistress pushed her way to the back, cowering behind her pupils.

"PLEASE DON'T EAT ME!" cried Miss Veer. "IT'S SPEECH DAY NEXT WEEK!"

"Don't worry, Mrs Headmistress!" said Winston. "This little fellow isn't going to eat you."

"That's a shame," mumbled one boy at the back.

"My pangolin friend here likes to eat ants."

The group all gazed intently as the zookeeper produced a jar of the little insects from out of his coat pocket. On seeing the delicious treats scuttling around behind the glass, the creature opened her mouth and her long, sticky tongue slithered out.

Poor Miss Veer looked alarmed.

"That is a very long tongue!" she murmured.

Next, Winston proceeded to pour the ants right on to the pangolin's tongue. She ate them all up greedily before rolling up into a ball. Not just any ball. An armour-plated ball.

"Oh no!" said Miss Veer.

Silence descended upon the children.

What was going to happen next?

The pangolin rolled herself up a ramp in her enclosure.

Then, from atop the aviary, Sir Basil boomed, "PANGOLIN! GO!"

On hearing those words, the creature rolled herself back down the ramp at speed.

Winston shouted, "BOB! JUMP!"

Just in time the boy jumped over the rolling pangolin, but the ball knocked over the three bullies standing behind him as if they were skittles. They were thrown into the air and one by one landed in the mud.

THUD!

THUD!!

THUD!!!

All the other children hooted with laughter at seeing these menaces being menaced.

"HA! HA! HA!"

The three bullies lay on the floor, dazed and confused, their bottoms all mucky.

Little did they know their ordeal was only just beginning.

CHAPTER TWELVE

ATTACK OF THE NOSES

Next, an extraordinary chain of events was set in motion by Sir Basil, with the help of Winston.

The zookeeper hurriedly began opening gates to the animal enclosures all around the zoo.

First, the hooded seal lumbered over and blew up his nose like a balloon.

"ARRRGGH!" yelled Stubbs, in fear of this strange creature. As he, Gaz and Baz backed away, they heard a roar behind them.

RRROARRRRRRR!!

They turned round to see the Komodo dragon doing her best dinosaur impression.

"ARRRGGH!" screamed the boys again.

As the trio backed away from the dragon, the umbrellabird attacked from above, whacking them on the back of their heads with his long wattle.

THWACK!

        THWACK!

                THWACK!

Despite priding themselves on being the toughest children in the school, the bullies all screamed, **"HELP!"**

But no help came.

It was as if Sir Basil was a conductor and the animals were his orchestra.

Next, the marabou stork took to the air, with three friends on board. The star-nosed mole was clinging on to one foot. The pig-nosed frog was gripping on to the other. The proboscis monkey was dingle-dangling from the stork's dingly-dangly neck.

**"D
R
O
P
!"**

boomed Sir Basil.

The three animals let go of the bird and fell through the air, landing one by one on top of the bullies' heads.

PLOP!

PLOP!

PLOP!

It was the attack of the noses!

The star-nosed mole tickled under Baz's chin with his wormy bits.

"HA! HA!" the boy laughed. But it was an agonising laugh. A laugh of pain. "No, no! I'm going to wet myself!"

The pig-nosed frog did a **MASSIVE** sneeze with her snout…

AAaaaaCHOOOOOO!

…and snotted into Gaz's face.

"AAAH! I can't see! I have frog snot in my eyes!"

Finally, the proboscis monkey shook his head from side to side, bashing Stubbs in the face with his long red hooter.

BAM! BAM! BAM!

"OW! OW! OW!" screamed Stubbs.

The children all shook with laughter.

"HA! HA! HA!"

But no one laughed louder than Bob.

"HA! HA! HA! HA! HA!"

"NO!" cried the headmistress. "THIS IS THE WORST SCHOOL TRIP EVER!"

But she was wrong. This was the best school trip ever.

CHAPTER THIRTEEN

A DROPPED BLANCMANGE

The three bullies stumbled around the zoo, desperate to find a way out. The dugong climbed the rocks at the side of her tank and took a giant leap into the water.

Moo!  SPLOSH!

The trio were soaked.

Baz started blubbing. "Why are all the animals picking on us?"

"NOW!" boomed Sir Basil again from the top of the aviary. Winston cleared the way through the crowds for the sloth, who for the first time ever was riding on the back of the tapir. Slowly but surely, the sloth slapped the tapir's bottom. As the tapir charged at the boys, the sloth looked very startled. She had never gone so fast in all her life.

The bullies retreated, only to be tripped up by the snapping turtle's shell. The three tumbled backwards, the turtle snapping at their heels as they fell.

SNAP! SNAP!

SNAP!

Gaz's bottom landed on the spikes on the echidna's back.

"AAAH!" the boy wailed.

Baz's bottom landed on the sharp tusks of the warthog. One tusk for each cheek.

"AAAAH!"

Stubbs glanced behind him. There was nothing for him to fall back on, so he looked smug. However, the hamadryas baboon leaped off the top of her enclosure and landed on the hooded seal's balloon-like nose.

BOING!

The baboon bounced up into the air…

WHOOSH!

Her bright red bottom went flying straight towards Stubbs's face… SPLAT!

"AAAAAAH!"

If you've never had a baboon's bottom in your face, I wouldn't recommend it. It's very overrated.

Gaz and Baz snorted with laughter.

"HO! HO! HO!"

The two henchmen thought they'd got away. They were wrong.

The elephant seal lolloped across the ground. Using his stumpy trunk, he scooped the three boys up one by one. As they desperately clung to the giant animal's back, he used his huge flippers to leap up into the air.

"HHHEEELLLPPPP!!!" screamed the boys.

The elephant seal landed in a water tank with a ginormous **SPLOSH!**

As the three boys' heads bobbed up, the spotted handfish swam towards them. The half-hand/half-fish shot out of the water and, with a series of leaps, slapped each one of the bullies around the face.

SLAP!
"OUCH!"

SLAP!!
"OUCH!!"

SLAP!!!
"OUCH!!!"

All three had big red handfish marks across their cheeks.

You might have thought this was plenty of humiliation, but no. There was still one more creature waiting for his chance to avenge Bob.

His friend Blob.

Bob beamed as he saw his special friend the blobfish leap from his tank into the spotted handfish's.

PLOP!

Stubbs, Baz and Gaz screamed in terror as the world's ugliest creature swam straight towards them.

The other children all looked on with interest. What was this fish, that looked like a dropped blancmange, going to do?

"GET AWAY FROM US!" cried the boys in terror.

"NOW!" ordered Sir Basil one last time.

First the blobfish swam up to Gaz, and gave him a big kiss on the lips.

"EURGH!" uttered the boy.

Next the blobfish swam up to Baz, and gave him an even bigger kiss on the lips.

"EURGH!"

Stubbs desperately tried to escape. He swam as far away as he could, and clung to the side of the tank.

One by one, the spotted handfish bent back the boy's fingers. Then the elephant seal hooked his trunk round the back of the boy's trousers and dragged him back into the middle of the tank.

Finally, the blobfish took a long swim-up* and sped through the water towards Stubbs. The boy tried to cry out, but it was impossible to make a sound. The blobfish had pushed his big, pink, blubbery lips right up against the boy's.

Their kiss made a noise like air slowly escaping from a balloon.

SQUEEEAAAK! The kiss was so strong that Stubbs passed out.

The boy lay motionless in the water.

"NOOOO!" cried Miss Veer.

*a fishy term for run-up

CHAPTER FOURTEEN

LICKED BACK TO LIFE

"This will not look good for Grottington!" spluttered the headmistress. "This will not look good at all. And we have the school inspectors coming next week! They're bound to notice if a child is missing!"

Winston tried to clamber up into the tank, but he lost his footing and landed in a heap in the mud.

"OOF!"

As much as Bob didn't like the bully, he didn't want to see him drown. He had to think fast.

He saw that the Komodo dragon was standing by Blob's tank. Remembering the time when the bullies had made him walk up a dinosaur's skeleton, he ran up the back of the Komodo dragon.

ROAR!

Then the boy leaped off the creature's head into the tank below.

SPLOSH!

Bob grabbed Stubbs under the chin and swam to the side of the tank. Gaz and Baz helped push their friend out of the water, and clambered to safety.

All the schoolchildren lifted Stubbs and laid him gently on the ground. Now they felt sorry for him. He was just a short little boy, after all.

The pangolin, no longer rolled up into a ball, pushed past the crowd. She stuck out her long, sticky tongue…

…and licked the boy back to life.

Slowly Stubbs came round. The bully opened his eyes, and looked surprised to see it was Bob who was helping him.

"Blob?" murmured Stubbs.

"It's Bob," corrected Bob.

"Sorry," said Stubbs, looking sheepish. "Thank you, Bob."

Bob helped Stubbs to his feet, and the two boys smiled at each other.

CHAPTER FIFTEEN

A SPLENDID DAY OUT

"What an absolutely splendid day out!" announced Miss Veer cheerily, trying to lighten the mood. "Children, I beg of you, please don't mention a word of this to your parents. I am only a year off retirement."

The children all nodded their heads and smirked. This had been the *best* day out.

"Now, no more bullying from you three," said Bob to Stubbs's gang. "Or you'll have this lot to answer to."

The boy indicated his army of animal friends, who all gathered together and scowled at the three bullies.

"We won't," said Stubbs, looking ashamed of himself.

"Definitely won't!" added Gaz.

"Won't what?" asked Baz.

A little while later, Miss Veer was leading her Grottington pupils out of the zoo. "Another completely incident-free school trip!" she said brightly.

Just as the party reached the gate, Sir Basil called Bob back.

"Bob!" The man was back on the ground now.

"Yes, sir?" replied the boy.

"I have a present for you. Winston?"

The zookeeper appeared with something hidden behind his back.

"What is it?" asked Bob excitedly.

"It's Blob!" announced Winston, as he revealed the funny-faced fish in a tank.

"BLOB!" shouted the boy, as he ran towards his friend and wrapped his arms round the tank.

Blob swam up to the glass and squashed his already squashed-up face against it.

"Now, young Bob, you need to promise me you'll take good care of him," said the zoo owner.

"So I can take him home?!" asked Bob.

"Yes," replied Sir Basil. "I know he'll be happiest with you, his best friend in all the world."

"Thank you! Thank you! Thank you!" exclaimed the boy.

"Animals can't talk," said Winston. "Well, not to us humans at least, but if Blob could, I know he'd be saying…"

"What?"

"'…I love you.'"

Bob looked at his new pet. "I wish I could tell him I love him too."

"He knows," replied Winston, with a smile.

EPILOGUE

Bob put Blob's tank in pride of place in his bedroom, on a box next to his bed.

Blob became part of the family. He ate his meals at the kitchen table with Bob and Grandpa. Sometimes Winston and Sir Basil would join them too.

On Sunday nights, Bob and Blob would even have a bath together.

Bob and Grandpa often took the fish out for a spin on the old man's mobility scooter.

Every afternoon after school, Grandpa would take his two grandsons, Bob and Blob, to the zoo. They had free entry for life. Blob always looked happy to see his animal friends and Winston again.

Every night the boy went to sleep staring at his friend.

They both had funny faces. It was the best thing in the world.

GLOSSARY

All the animals in this story are real. You can learn more about them here.

AYE-AYE: is a type of lemur. It's nocturnal, which means it likes to come out at night.

BLOBFISH: lives at depths of between 2,000 to 4,000 metres. Its body is jelly-like so it can survive so far underwater without being crushed. It looks very different at the surface than it would do at the bottom of the sea, because down there the weight of the water squashes it into a more fishlike shape. It was recently voted the world's ugliest animal.

DUGONG: is called a "sea cow" as it feeds mainly on seagrass. It has been hunted by humans for centuries, and now faces extinction.

ECHIDNA: eats ants and termites, and is one of only two mammals that lay eggs.

ELEPHANT SEAL: is a large earless seal that lives in the ocean. It can hold its breath for a hundred minutes!

HAMADRYAS BABOON: was a sacred animal to the ancient Egyptians. It's sometimes called the "sacred baboon". You can tell a male from a female as only males have a fur cape.

 HOODED SEAL: feeds in very deep waters, sometimes between 100 and 600 metres down, and spends most of its time in the sea. The male has an inflatable hood that it uses for communication and showing off.

KOMODO DRAGON: is actually a very big lizard. It eats mainly meat – like deer – and has been known to attack humans.

MARABOU STORK: has one of the largest wingspans of any bird – nearly three metres. It eats fish, frogs and even crocodile eggs.

PANGOLIN: has large protective scales all over its skin. It lives in hollow trees or burrows under the ground. It only comes out at night, and eats mostly ants and termites.

PROBOSCIS MONKEY: communicates using honks. There is a special honk to reassure baby proboscis monkeys. "Proboscis" is a scientific word for nose.

PURPLE PIG-NOSED FROG: can be found in India. It's much rounder than other frogs. It spends most of its life underground, but comes up at monsoon (rainstorm) time for mating.

 **SLOTH:** is so slow that it likes to stay up trees where it is safer. It is one of the sleepiest animals in the world, napping for between fifteen to twenty hours a day.

SNAPPING TURTLE: is so called for its beak-like jaws. It tends to hide quietly when in the water, but often snaps when out of it.

 SPOTTED HANDFISH: is a very rare type of fish found in the seas around Tasmania. It prefers to walk on the seabed rather than swim.

STAR-NOSED MOLE: uses those twenty-two appendages as an eye to find its way around. You might see one in North America.

TAPIR: lives in jungles and forests. It likes to cool off in water, and can happily walk along a riverbed underwater.

UMBRELLABIRD: is found in the rainforests of Central and South America. The wattle on its neck makes its booming calls louder.

WARTHOG: is a type of pig that you would find in Africa. It eats mainly plants and bugs.

More brilliant books by David Walliams

HAPPY BIRTHDAY WORLD BOOK DAY!

Let's celebrate . . .

Can you believe this year is our **20th birthday** – and thanks to you, as well as our amazing authors, illustrators, booksellers, librarians and teachers, there's SO much to celebrate!

Did you know that since WORLD BOOK DAY began in 1997, we've given away over **275 million book tokens**? WOW! We're delighted to have brought so many books directly into the hands of millions of children and young people just like you, with a gigantic assortment of fun activities and events and resources and quizzes and dressing-up and games too – we've even broken a **Guinness World Record**!

Whether you love discovering books that make you **laugh**, CRY, *hide under the covers* or **drive your imagination wild**, with WORLD BOOK DAY, there's always something for everyone to choose–as well as ideas for exciting new books to try at bookshops, libraries and schools everywhere.

And as a small charity, we couldn't do it without a lot of help from our friends in the publishing industry and our brilliant sponsor, NATIONAL BOOK TOKENS. Hip-hip hooray to them and three cheers to you, our readers and everyone else who has joined us over the last 20 years to make WORLD BOOK DAY happen.

Happy Birthday to us – and happy reading to you!

Illustrations © Liz Pichon

#WorldBookDay20

BOOK IN
FOR YOUR NEW ADVENTURE TODAY

CELEBRATING

WORLD **BOOK** DAY

20 2 MARCH 2017

3 brilliant ways to continue YOUR reading adventure

1 VISIT YOUR LOCAL BOOKSHOP

Your go-to destination for awesome reading recommendations and events with your favourite authors and illustrators.

 FIND YOUR LOCAL BOOKSHOP **Booksellers.org.uk/ bookshopsearch**

2 JOIN YOUR LOCAL LIBRARY

Browse and borrow from a huge selection of books, get expert ideas of what to read next, and take part in wonderful family reading activities – all for FREE!

FIND YOUR LOCAL LIBRARY **Findalibrary.co.uk**

3 DISCOVER A WORLD OF STORIES ONLINE

32 podcasts to try

Stuck for ideas of what to read next? Plug yourself in to our brilliant new podcast library! Sample a world of amazing books, brought to life by amazing storytellers. **worldbookday.com**